Where Do Insects Live?

Susan Canizares • Mary Reid

Scholastic Inc.
New York • Toronto • London • Auckland • Sydney

Acknowledgments

Science Consultants: Patrick R. Thomas, Ph.D., Bronx Zoo/Wildlife Conservation Park; Glenn Phillips, The New York Botanical Garden; **Literacy Specialist:** Maria Utefsky Reading Recovery Coordinator, District 2, New York City

Design: MKR Design, Inc.

Photo Research: Barbara Scott

Endnotes: Susan Russell

Photographs: Cover: Alan & Linda Detrick/Photo Researchers, Inc.; p. 1: Robert & Linda Mitchell; p. 2: C.A. Henley; p. 3: Joe McDonald/DRK Photo; p. 4: Hans Pfletschinger/Peter Arnold, Inc.; p. 5: Hermann Eisenbeiss/Photo Researchers, Inc.; p. 6: Joe McDonald/DRK Photo; p. 7: Michael Fogden/DRK Photo; p. 8: John J. Dommers/Photo Researchers, Inc.; p. 9: Rod Planck/Photo Researchers, Inc.; p. 10: Robert & Linda Mitchell; p. 11: Stephen Dalton/Photo Researchers, Inc.; p. 12: James L. Amos/Peter Arnold, Inc.

Library of Congress Cataloging-in-Publication Data
Canizares, Susan, 1960-
Where do insects live? / Susan Canizares, Mary Reid.
p. cm. -- (Science emergent readers)
"Scholastic early childhood."--P. [4] of cover.
Includes index.
Summary: Photographs and simple text describe the habitats of different insects.
ISBN 0-590-39793-1 (pbk.: alk. paper)
1. Insects--Habitat--Juvenile literature. 2. Insect--Habitations--Juvenile literature. [1. Insects--Habitat.]
I. Reid, Mary. II. Title. III. Series.
QL467.2.C357 1998
595.7--dc21   97-29201
                                                                                                     CIP AC

20   19   18   17   16   15   14   13   12   03   02   01   00

Where do insects live?

In the grass.

On a tree.

On a leaf.

On a rock.

In the sand.

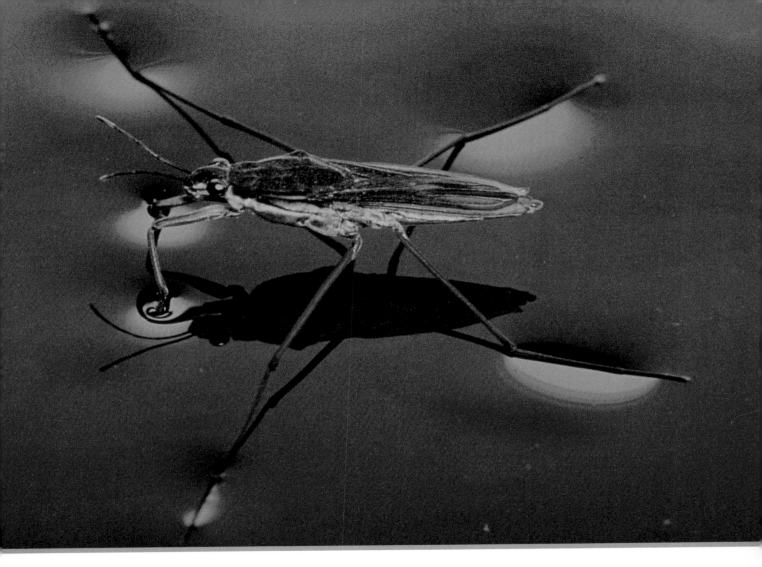

On the water.

On a log.

In a hole.

In a nest.

In the air.

Insects live everywhere!

Where Do Insects Live?

Insects live all around us. They live in our houses and in the fields. They thrive in water, in the forests, in the driest deserts, and in warm climates and cold. They even live in the Arctic! Insects know how to live very well. They are the most successful creatures on earth.

The Weaver Ant pictured here is standing in the opening of the nest that has been built out of leaves. The adult ants work together to sew shelters out of the delicate silk that comes from the larvae.

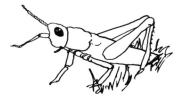

The Grasshopper (left) lives in grass or fields that often have the same coloration. It relies on its jumping ability to escape from enemies, leaping up to 20 times its body length! The Treehopper (right) lives in trees or on twigs, where it looks just like a thorn. It eats the sap of the plant.

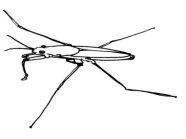

The Shield Bug (left), one of a large family of bugs, eats plants and can produce a very bad smell. It can be a pest for farmers. The Water Strider (right) has a fan of tiny hairs at the tips of its legs that act like "snowshoes," letting it skate along the surface of the water to find food.

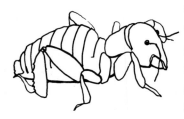

There are many varieties of cricket (left). This Jerusalem Cricket lives under rocks and makes a scratchy noise. The Stone Grasshopper (right) lives in rocky territory and is perfectly camouflaged where it is sitting.

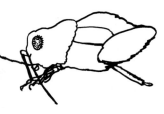

Carpenter Ants (left) drill deep into wood to nest and lay their eggs. They don't eat the wood like termites, but still can cause a great deal of damage. The ant burrows (right) are the doorways to large underground communities of ants. Each ant has a special job in these organized groups.

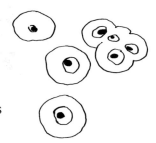

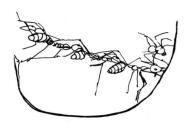

The Weaver Ants (left) are shown working together as they sew leaves into shelters. One group holds the edges of the leaf in place while others secure it. The Monarch Butterfly (right) literally lives in the air, flying 2,000 miles from Canada to Mexico and back. It often comes to the same resting places along the way.